bowmar   gallimaufry · book four

The great bell of Peking
and other stories by Margaret Greaves

illustrated by Jill McDonald · design and lettering by Paul Taylor

Gallimaufry is a very old word. It's a good word to use when you want to name a hodge-podge or mixture of all sorts of things. Your Gallimaufry Books contain a marvelous mixture of ancient and modern stories, serious and funny happenings—and sometimes magic. You'll find this mixture of stories is all about people, about trying to understand them and ourselves, about oddities and ambitions and rivalries and courage, about the things we value and the things we fear . . .

American edition 1975 BOWMAR®, Glendale, California 91201

Printed in the United States of America
International Standard Book Number 0-8372-1053-4
Library of Congress Catalog Card Number 74-10326

First published in England by Methuen Educational Ltd.
Text © 1971 Margaret Greaves
Illustrations © 1971 Methuen Educational Ltd.

1 2 3 4 5 6 7 8 9 84 83 82 81 80 79 78 77 76 75

Contents

The great bell of Peking

"I have made Peking the most beautiful city in China," said the great Emperor Yung-Lo. "I have built temples and palaces. I have laid out gardens brilliant with flowers and birds, and bright with fountains, like the gardens of heaven. The houses are fine and prosperous, and the streets gay with almond blossom. Without doubt, there is no other city like it in the world."

His Chief Counselor, Ming-Lin, smiled. It was not a pleasant smile, for Ming-Lin was thin and gray and bitter, and he had eyes like a snake's. He looked a little sideways at the Emperor, then nodded three times very politely.

"Indeed, Son of Heaven, most magnificent Majesty," he agreed. "It is the most beautiful city on earth. It lacks only one thing to make it perfect."

"What is that?" demanded the Emperor, angry that any fault at all could be found.

"It needs a bell," said Ming-Lin. "A great bell, golden-voiced like a god, a great bell that all the city may hear, to sound the hours of prayer and rest. Every time it rings, its voice will seem to say, 'Praise to the Emperor Yung-Lo, the Son of Heaven.'"

The Emperor was well pleased. "You speak wisely as ever, Ming-Lin. Such a bell would be the crown and glory of all my work. But where shall I find a craftsman to cast one fine enough?"

"Kwan-Yu, your Majesty's chief cannon-maker, is the man," advised Ming-Lin. "There is no better craftsman in the kingdom."

But Ming-Lin's praise was like a secret dagger in the back of an enemy. He hated Kwan-Yu, whom the Emperor had often honored; and he knew that, much as Kwan-Yu knew about cannon, he had no knowledge of the making of bells. Thus Ming-Lin hoped to destroy him.

The delighted Emperor sent at once for Kwan-Yu. He explained what he desired, and smiled most graciously. "And you, our finest craftsman, shall have the honor of making such a wonder."

Kwan-Yu went white and stared at the bitter gray face of Ming-Lin, who stood smiling behind the Emperor's shoulder. He knew that he was undone, for when the Emperor commanded, none dared refuse.

"Your Majesty honors this poor person too highly," he said, in a voice stony with despair. "But so great a work will take time. Grant me a full year in which to do it. Also the cost will be very great, for I must have gold and brass, silver and iron, all in huge quantities.

But the Emperor was not deterred.

"All these things you shall have, and everything else you require. A year from today we will watch the final casting. If it is good, you shall command what you will as a reward. If it should fail, your life will pay the penalty."

He rose from his throne, in his dragon robes of black and red and gold, and swept from the room, while Kwan-Yu lay prostrate as he passed.

For six months Kwan-Yu consulted every book

and traveled up and down the kingdom, learning everything he could about the casting of bells. Then he began work; yet he knew in his heart he was doomed to fail.

His beloved daughter, Ko-ai, watched her father with sad and anxious eyes. She knew about his trouble, though always he assured her affectionately that all was well. She grew thin and pale with long anxiety, and each day she went to the temple to pray for his success.

The year slipped by, and the day of the casting came. The Emperor and his whole court appeared to watch it. In a huge open space stood the giant earthenware mold all ready to receive the precious metals. Beside it was the vast caldron in which the molten mass seethed slowly with a dull and dangerous sheen. Everything was ready. The Emperor raised his hand.

Slowly the great caldron was tilted forward. Slowly the glowing metals poured themselves into the mold. But something was wrong. Gold, brass, iron, silver—the discordant elements refused to mix. There was a mighty crack, dull and heavy in sound, and the earthen mold split to its very base.

Dark with anger, the Emperor rose to give judgment. Attendants flung Kwan-Yu at his feet, and the black-masked executioner stood by with upraised axe. Kwan-Yu uttered no sound, for he expected no mercy. But Ko-ai sprang from her place among the other maidens and cast herself imploringly at the Emperor's feet.

"Mercy! Oh be merciful, Son of Heaven!
Greatness consists in mercy. Let my father live and
try once more."

Touched by her beauty and devotion, the
Emperor slowly dropped his hands and held them
palm upwards in the gesture of mercy.

"For your daughter's sake," he said to the
trembling craftsman, "you shall have another half
year. But if you fail again, your life shall pay for it."

But what use was six months to one who had
not the secret of the art? Though father and
daughter tried to cheer each other, their grief grew
heavier and heavier as the fatal day approached.
All indeed happened as they foresaw. The seething
metals ran into the great mold, but nothing united
them, and once again the six months labor was
spoiled.

This time the Emperor's fury knew no bounds,
and Ming-Lin watched in secret triumph. In his
rage and disappointment it seemed as if the
Emperor might almost kill the unhappy craftsman
with his own hands. But once again Ko-ai flung
herself across her father's body, just beneath the
dreadful axe, and begged with tears for his life. At
last the Emperor's heart was moved again, and he
pardoned Kwan-Yu for the second time. But he
swore a great oath by the gods, which even he
dared never break, that no other mercy would ever
be given. The bell must be cast six months from
that very day.

For many weeks, as her father grew thin with

despair, Ko-ai went about her household tasks in silence and tears. But one day, as she was returning from her daily prayers in the temple, a little bird perched and fluttered and sang on a branch that grew close to her path.

"Thank you, little bird," she said very gently, "for I'm sure you are trying to comfort me."

"Ko-ai," said the bird, "I bring you comfort indeed, if you have the courage to take it. The gods have heard your many prayers for your father. Today a very great magician is visiting his mother in the village down in the valley there. Seek him out and he will tell you what to do."

Ko-ai could hardly believe her ears. But she bowed very humbly to the little blue bird as to a messenger of the gods. The creature fluttered away, and she hurried joyously down the mountain path to the village. The great magician seemed to expect her coming.

"I know your grief, Ko-ai," he said, "and will seek the counsel of the gods."

Into a bowl that changed colors like the sky he poured oil of almonds, the dew of flowers, powdered deer-horn, and other strange ingredients. Last of all he added two small drops of serpent's blood, and a pale cloudy vapor began to steam up from the bowl. The magician watched until the last of the smoke had drifted away. Then he turned to Ko-ai and took her hands, looking down at her sternly yet kindly.

"Iron for strength, brass for endurance, silver for

sweetness, gold for music—what can unite such unlike substances? Daughter, must you indeed know the answer to your question?"

Looking into his eyes, Ko-ai nodded, for she dared not speak.

"Only one thing in this world can do it, my daughter. The life of a maiden, freely given."

And Ko-ai went slowly and silently away.

At last came the day for the final test. The Emperor, dark and stern in his dragon robes, waited grimly on his throne. The empty mold stood waiting. The smooth hot metals bubbled together in the great caldron. Near it stood Ko-ai in her brightest garments, her hair full of flowers, her best jeweled slippers on her little feet. As Kwan-Yu, resigned to death, raised his hand in the last signal to the workmen, she sprang forward with a cry.

"For my father's life, O gods, I come to you!"

Swift as a bird she leaped, in one bright jeweled flash, into the dull gleam of the waiting metal.

There was a cry of horror and amazement from all around as the dark liquid closed over her slender body and began to run into the waiting mold. At that same moment, a bright blue bird skimmed from its surface away into the sky and was lost forever to the sight.

For the last time, the metals poured into their home, and this time there was no fault. As they settled and cooled, everyone could see how smoothly they united—iron for strength, brass for endurance, silver for sweetness, and gold for music.

The Emperor looked at the distracted father, and bowed his head as if to an equal.

"You and your daughter have triumphed, Kwan-Yu. Choose what you will for a reward."

"Son of Heaven," said Kwan-Yu, "give me, I pray you, the life of your Chief Counselor, Ming-Lin."

The Emperor raised his hand, and Ming-Lin threw himself in the dust at his enemy's feet. The executioner raised his axe.

"Stay," said Kwan-Yu. "If my daughter lived, she would beg for your life. It is hers, not mine. Go."

And Ming-Lin rose and walked very slowly from the Emperor's presence. No one ever saw him again.

When the great bell was cooled and hung, it rang for the first time over the city, golden-voiced and strong and true. The listening Emperor laid his hand on the shoulder of Kwan-Yu, who now served him as Chief Counselor, and looked around at all his courtiers.

"Ming-Lin said that the great bell would praise the Emperor each time it rang. Tell me, one of you," he demanded, "is it my name that is praised?"

For a long while the courtiers were silent, afraid to speak. Then a very old man raised his head.

"Majesty, Son of Heaven, it is not your name that the bell speaks but another's. Listen to its voice—Ko-ai, Ko-ai."

Humbly the Emperor bowed to him.

"Wisely and bravely spoken," he said. "As long as the great bell rings over Peking, may the people forget the Emperor Yung-Lo, and honor the courage and the love of Ko-ai."

And so it was. Day after day, for the hours of prayer and rest, the golden voice of the great bell sounded over Peking, over the palaces and gardens and the streets full of almond blossom—"Ko-ai, Ko-ai!"—long after the Emperor and the Emperor's son and his son's son after him had died and been forgotten.

"Ko-ai,
     Ko-ai,
          Ko-ai."

Traditional

Switchback

The fair seemed like an explosion of light and noise against the dark sky above it. The three boys stared at the poster of the Strong Man while Harry fumbled for his spending money.

"If I were as strong as that I'd be a boxer," said John.

"I wouldn't," said Harry. I'd be a policeman. I'd be the biggest policeman in the country."

"I'd be a lion tamer," said Cyril.

"You wouldn't," said John. "If a lion scratched you, you'd cry at the blood."

Cyril kicked a stone and said nothing. It was true, he hated blood. He had no father or brothers and sisters, and his mother worried so much about him that he worried about himself. He tried to whistle to show that he didn't care, but he wasn't very good at it.

Harry found his money, and they forgot about the Strong Man.

"Let's go on the dodgems first," John shouted above the noise.

They were just in time to get a car each before the machine started. John and Harry zigzagged madly across the middle of the floor, chasing each other and shouting with excitement whenever they collided. Cyril circled on the outside, close to the wall, and dodged everyone else rather skillfully. The music roared, the cars went faster, the light bulbs blurred into an orange glare. Nearly everyone seemed to be shouting. It was all glory.

Only too soon their turn was over.

"Now for the switchback," said Harry. "Come on quick! It's filling up."

They broke into a run, twisting between people and dogs and stalls. Someone pushed against Cyril and he fell sprawling against the side of a cotton candy counter. There was a sudden sharp pain in his knee. He pressed it as he scrambled up, and his fingers came away wet.

"Harry! John!" he shouted. "Wait for me. I hurt myself."

But his voice was lost in the din all around him. The boys didn't hear him. Everyone in the crowd was intent on all the excitements of the fair. No one even noticed a boy with an injured knee. The others were almost out of sight when Cyril pulled himself together and hurried limping after them, afraid of losing them in the crowd.

"I've hurt my knee," he yelled again as he caught

up with them at the switchback. But they were already climbing in, and he scrambled to a seat beside them. Dizzy, excited, he clung on among the whirl of lights and shouts and laughter, as they hurtled up and down, up and down, above the pale blur of faces on the ground below. There was no time to remember the pain in his knee.

When it was over, they walked away to the quieter edge of the fair. They had no more money to spend. Cyril's knee had stiffened and felt sore as the wind blew against it. Suddenly John noticed it.

"Wow!" he said. "Just look at your leg, Cyril. What on earth did you do?"

"I just bumped it," said Cyril. "On the way to the switchback."

"But you never said anything," said Harry. "It must have hurt like anything."

"There's an awful lot of blood," added John admiringly.

"It's all right," said Cyril, wiping some of the sticky stuff away as casually as he could.

"You'd better go home and get it washed," advised John. "You could come back afterwards."

Cyril nodded. "Maybe I'd better. See you later, then."

He turned away towards the quietness of the road beyond the fairground. His knee was really hurting now, but he managed to walk with a slight swagger.

Tomorrow he would get John to teach him how to whistle properly.

First impressions

I know now that it's stupid to jump to conclusions, but I learned it the hard way.

We won't forget the first week that Martin Buckroyd arrived in the village. From the orchard across the road, screened by the apple trees, we watched the new doctor and his family moving into their house. First came the furniture van—good, solid rather shabby furniture, and boxes and boxes of books.

"Goodness!" said Rosemary. "I wonder who reads all that?"

Then came a rather old family car, and the doctor himself got out. He was tall and grayish and looked, as Tim said, a bit grim.

"*I* think he looks rather sad," said Jane. But we all told her to shut up and not be so mushy.

A plump cheerful little woman, obviously the doctor's wife, got out of the car next. And then came a tall thin boy about my own age.

"Hooray," said Peter. "We can use someone else in the gang." He gave a long soft whistle, just to see what would happen.

The boy was standing nearest to us and must have heard it, but he never even turned his head. He took a bag out of the car and went straight indoors.

"Well!" I said, a bit angrily. The village is a friendly place, and we weren't used to being snubbed.

"I don't think he really noticed," said Jane. "Perhaps he's got something on his mind."

"All those books," giggled Rosemary.

We waited for a bit, but nothing seemed to happen. The doctor talked to the moving men and then they drove away. No one else came out of the house. It grew dusk and chilly, and we all went home.

We saw nothing of the newcomers for a couple of days after that. Then Tim and I met the boy face to face outside the Post Office.

"Hello," I said.

The boy gave a quick half-smile, glanced from me to Tim, and seemed to hesitate. Then he flushed painfully, nodded, and walked straight on. Tim stared after him, open-mouthed, then turned to me with almost a bellow of rage.

"Can you beat that? Of all the stupid, stuck-up, toffee-nosed bean-poles! Who does he think he is, I'd like to know!"

"Calm down," I said. But I was angry myself, and found nearly as many adjectives as Tim when we told the others about it.

"Just because he's the doctor's son," said Tim furiously, "I suppose he thinks he's better than we are."

"Maybe he's shy," suggested Peter.

Tim and I both made a rude noise.

"Well, he could be," protested Jane. She and Peter always stick up for each other.

"I don't believe it," said Rosemary. "He's too old to be shy. I vote we teach him a lesson."

We all agreed. Peter and Jane hesitated a bit, but they usually do what we say.

The next morning we all hung around near the duckpond. It's close to the doctor's house, and we figured he'd have to come out some time. He did.

Tim stood in his way, and raised his cap. (I don't know where he'd found one.)

"Good morning," he said, in an affected grown-up voice.

Rosemary giggled, a bit uneasily. The boy looked at Tim, with his odd hesitating manner, and said, "Hello," uncertainly. He didn't seem to notice the rest of us, who were grinning away in the background. He nodded and went straight on, and Tim, whose temper is never very guarded, felt snubbed and went scarlet with rage.

"All right then, come on!" he cried savagely to the rest of us. "Left, right. Left, right."

We fell into line behind the doctor's son, keeping in step with him, slapping our feet down hard upon the road. "Good morning," said Tim, in time to our footsteps, goading the others into a chorus. "Good morning, good morning, good morning."

I ought to have stopped it then, of course. I had a feeling there was something wrong. But we were all a bit hurt and angry. And when even this demonstration had no effect upon the boy, Tim lost his temper entirely. Before we could see what he was going to do, he had bent down, picked up a stone, and thrown it.

It was only a very small stone. Even Tim had that much sense. But it caught the boy right between the shoulders. He stopped dead, and there was a second's pause that seemed like minutes. I saw Tim's face and was sorry for him. I knew just how much he wished he hadn't done it.

Then slowly the boy turned. He saw the five of us, standing in a group in the road. We must have looked pretty silly too, though we tried to stare him down.

The boy came towards us. To our astonishment, he was smiling as if at friends, although the color in his face was high and he spoke very shyly.

"Hi," he said. "Did you really want to speak to me? I'm sorry, I didn't know. Most people don't want to talk. I'm deaf, you know."

A secret place

Stephen found it first. Aunt Louise and Aunt Meg had given each of them a chocolate bar and sent them out to look around.

"Have a lovely time," said Aunt Louise. "We do want you children to enjoy yourselves while you're with us."

"Thank you," said Marcia politely. "I'm sure we shall."

"Go exploring," went on Aunt Louise brightly. "You never know what you'll find, do you?"

"No," agreed Marcia, suddenly depressed. She had been thinking the same thing herself, but it sounded quite different in Aunt Louise's "I-know-what-children-like" voice.

"What does she think we'll find?" demanded Harry crossly, when they were out of earshot. "Fairies in the bottom of the garden?"

They passed the kitchen window. Aunt Meg looked out from behind the sink.

"Hello," she said. "Will baked potatoes in their jackets suit you for lunch?"

"Hooray," shouted Harry. They went on their way, much cheered.

They wandered across two fields. In one was an old shed, and they spent some time poking around, but found nothing very exciting. At the bottom of the next field was a stream.

"Let's each take a different spot," suggested Stephen, "and see if there are any good fishing places. I'll start at that tree."

He ran ahead. They saw him stop at the tree and look around, steadying himself with a hand on the trunk. Then he took a step forward and suddenly disappeared.

"Goodness!" Marcia broke into a run. "He must have fallen in. I wonder if it's deep."

They sprinted down to the tree, and then stopped dead. Stephen hadn't fallen in. He was standing at the bottom of a steep bank. At its base was a small shelf of gravel sloping to the stream. A fallen branch of the great tree lay across it. Primroses clung to little hollows where roots twisted through the soil of the bank and made footholds for them to climb down. The bank, higher than their heads, cut off the fields from view; and one side of it was further screened by a thicket of bright hawthorn.

"A *secret* place!" said Harry with satisfaction.

They spent the whole morning there. It was their fortress, their camp, their hiding-place. Then they remembered the baked potatoes and hurried back just in time for lunch.

"Where have you been?" asked Aunt Louise with enthusiastic interest. She always wanted to know where they had been.

"Oh, out," said Stephen vaguely.

"Out's a big place," said Aunt Louise archly, ready to pursue the subject, but Aunt Meg broke in.

"How can they tell where they've been," she said reasonably, "when they don't know where anything is? Another potato, Marcia?"

So it was still a secret place. They asked for a picnic, and later ate it sitting in a friendly row on the fallen branch. From her end of the branch, Marcia could just reach to put her feet in the stream.

For the next two or three days they explored the neighborhood, but always came back to the little den below the great tree. They could fish there, or talk, or read, or just mess around, entirely undisturbed. No one else knew about the secret place.

One warm sunny morning at the end of the week, Stephen was reading peacefully on the fallen branch. Marcia was picking primroses, and Harry was still trying to drop a pebble on one of the minnows. Suddenly a human voice broke through the rustle of leaves and stream water.

"Coo-eee! Coo-coo-eee!"

The children looked at each other in dismay. Unmistakeably it was Aunt Louise.

"Coo-coo-eee!" The voice came nearer. Then she was standing on the top of the bank, smiling brightly down at them. "*There* you are! I had a feeling you might be down by the stream. What a lovely place you've found!"

"Yes, isn't it," said Marcia lamely.

Stephen closed his book and slipped it into his pocket. Harry stood up.

"It's perfect, isn't it," went on Aunt Louise with enthusiasm. "A little private place all of your own. It's a perfect place for a picnic too. I tell you what—why don't you invite Aunt Meg and me to a picnic this afternoon? I think there's still an old beach tent in the attic. You could have that to use for playing Indians. You'd like that, wouldn't you?"

"We *love* playing Indians," said Harry in Aunt Louise's voice.

Marcia stepped firmly on his foot.

"It's very kind of you, Aunt Louise," she said. "Of course it would be nice to have a picnic."

"Lovely," said Aunt Louise. It seemed to be her favorite word.

She went back to the house to look for the tent, and the children turned back to the stream. But somehow it wasn't the same. They trailed back to lunch a little earlier than usual.

It was a slightly awkward picnic. It was embarrassing to play Indians with Aunt Louise as Minni-ha-ha. But Aunt Meg had made some extremely good currant scones as well as chocolate biscuits and ginger cake, so really it wasn't all bad. Stephen helped Aunt Meg pack up afterwards.

"It was a good place to find," said Aunt Meg.

"Yes," agreed Stephen, a bit flatly.

"When I was young," said Aunt Meg, "I used to use the other side of the stream. You can get to it over the bridge down the lane. There are some good places there too. But they're very difficult to climb down to."

She grinned at him suddenly as she put the food away.

The next day, when they all came back to lunch, Aunt Louise greeted them brightly.

"Did you have a good morning?" she inquired. "Have you been to your secret place again?"

They all smiled at her warmly.

"Yes," said Stephen.

There was red mud on their shoes instead of gravel. But fortunately Aunt Louise didn't notice.

The Bishop and the beggar

Many hundreds of years ago, when the countryside
was wild and dangerous, six men were riding down
a long and lonely road. The raw November dusk
was nearly on them, and the cold rain had soaked
right through the brown woolen cloaks that they
pulled so closely around them. They shivered as
they rode, and longed for the warmth and shelter
of the great house just ahead. Only Germanus, the
good Bishop, still seemed cheerful.

They cast sharp glances from side to side, alert
to every shadow—even so near to a house, each
tree might hide a robber or a wild beast hungrier
than themselves. Suddenly one of the men shouted
and his horse swerved aside as a dark figure slipped
into the road. But it was only a half-naked scarecrow
of a beggar hoping for alms. The men would have
hurried on past him, but the Bishop halted.

"Wait!" he said sternly. "Do you call yourselves
Christian men? You have warm cloaks to cover
you, but our brother here has nothing but rags and
holes. You have eaten today, but he is starved.
You ride good horses, but he has not even shoes
for his feet. He shall come with us tonight."

Ashamed, one of the men reached down his hand
and helped the astonished beggar to mount behind
him. In a very few minutes they reached the
shelter of the abbey where they were expected.

That night the beggar had the best meal he had
ever known. He exchanged his old rags for good
warm clothes, and slept in comfort for the first
time in his life. Bishop Germanus also slept soundly,
thankful that he had been able to help a fellow man.

When the Bishop came down to the courtyard
the next morning, ready to continue his journey,

a servant brought him a new horse.

"What is this?" asked Germanus. "Where is my own gray horse? I never ride any other."

The servant looked troubled and angry.

"Alas, my lord," he said. "That beggar to whom you were so good—he stole away early in the morning and took your horse with him. Little he deserved such kindness! I wish I could lay my hands on him!"

But the Bishop's face was sad.

"Every man in need deserves kindness," he said. "There must have been some fault in me."

He stood for a moment as if listening, and then suddenly he smiled.

"None the less," he said, "I think we may see my horse again. Let us ride slowly on."

He mounted the new horse, and the little group of riders swung out of the courtyard. The weather had cleared, sunshine flooded the pale blue of the wintry sky. It was a good day for a gallop, but the Bishop kept his horse to a foot-pace, and still seemed to listen. And then the other men too heard the sound for which he was waiting. Far down the road behind them came the thud of hooves.

The Bishop halted and turned, giving a low soft whistle. A delighted whinny answered him, and around the last curve in the road came a single rider on a gray horse, galloping fast to catch up to them. The next moment the beggar had flung himself to the ground and was kneeling at the Bishop's feet, while the gray horse nuzzled against his hand.

"Pardon, my lord Bishop, pardon!" implored the beggar. "I did indeed try to steal your horse, but he would not come. He wouldn't budge a foot out of earshot of the abbey, so we hid in the trees until you had gone."

30

"That's my beauty," said the Bishop softly,
fondling the ears of the gray horse.

"The dumb beast showed me what a beast I
was," said the beggar humbly. "He loves you too
much to leave you, but I, wretch that I am, stole
from you after all your kindness."

Germanus shook his head.

"Indeed, my friend," he said, "the fault was
mine. Had I given you a horse, you need not have
stolen. The gray will never leave me—for it is true
that I love him, and he me—but this one will call
you master." He swung down from the horse he sat
on and put the bridle in the beggar's hand.

"Take him, my friend, and use him well, and
blessings go with you."

While the man stammered his thanks, Germanus
helped him to mount—turning the horse with a
slap on its flank to send it back the way it had
come. Then he mounted his own gray horse again.
His companions gathered their reins, ready to move
on. But the Bishop sat where he was for a while,
gazing back down the road, until the distant rider
and his horse were no bigger than a black crow in
the pale sunshine of the winter fields.

Medieval story

31

The treasure

Christine hummed to herself as she pranced through the Gardens. The sun shone warmly through her cotton shirt. The air was filled with the smell of trodden grass and red and yellow dahlias licked at the park railings like little hot flames. She had a whole dime to spend, and Mother was home from work today too.

Christine kept one hand in her pocket, her fingers curled over her latest treasure brought back from a holiday. It was a piece of quartz. One side, smoothed by the endless washing of the sea, felt warm and almost powdery to the touch. She took it out and looked at the black streaks crossing the dull sunset color of its more jagged surface. When she held it towards the sun, the whole piece glittered with hundreds of tiny stars. Almost like diamonds, she thought. Lovingly she slipped it back into her pocket, but kept it still in her hand.

The Gardens were full of pleasant sound. Voices drifted over the grass, somewhere a bat knocked against a ball, a robin trickled his thin sweet notes from the leaves of the nearest tree. But something was wrong. Muffled at first, then piercingly loud, came the outraged wailing of a small child. It was a sound that always gave Christine a sort of pain in her stomach. It had to be stopped.

She hurried around the next bend in the path. A very small girl sat in a heap on the ground where she had fallen trying to climb on a seat. She had bumped her knee and elbow but was more upset than hurt. As Christine ran to pick her up, she roared more loudly than ever and pushed at her with fat starfish hands.

"There, there!" soothed Christine. "It's all right."

But the child struggled on her lap still angry with the whole world.

"Look at the flowers," said Christine anxiously, still trying to distract her.

The child stopped, but only for breath, and let out another yell. Some boys were kicking a ball not far away, but no one else was near. Desperately Christine brought out her precious piece of quartz and held it to the light.

"Look!" she said. "Diamonds!"

The child stopped, reached out both hands, and grabbed.

"Pretty," she said. "Pretty." She climbed down to the grass, clutching the stone to her, and began to play with it. Her tears dried. When she seemed happy again, Christine bent down to pick up her treasure.

But it was not so easy. The child snatched it back from her.

"Mine," she protested. "Mine."

"No," said Christine. "I only loaned it to you. Let me have it. That's a good girl."

But the baby was not going to be a good girl. Her lip trembled. Christine picked up a big leaf that lay near and tried to interest her in it while she took back her stone. But as soon as she touched the quartz again the child let out a yell of anger and dismay.

Christine struggled with herself. She wanted to keep her treasure, but the baby apparently wanted it just as much. With a sigh she left it where it was.

"All right," she said. "You have it."

As she got up to go, she saw that one of the boys was coming over attracted at last by the child's final yell. She walked away, but turned her head after a few yards to see that all was well.

34

The boy bent down and put a toffee candy in the little girl's mouth.

"Here," he said with casual kindness. "Someone been bothering you? We'll go back to Mom now, shall we?"

He pulled her to her feet and the piece of quartz fell from her lap.

"What have you got?" asked the boy. He picked it up, turned it over, and dropped it. "It's only a silly old stone," he said, kicking it away down the path. "Come along, Lil."

The child took his hand and trotted off with him, without even a backward glance. When they had gone, Christine walked slowly back to where her late treasure lay forgotten. She turned it over with her foot. Was that what it was—only a silly old stone? She stood there, looking down at it.

Snow

I grow old. It seems more than twenty years since
the Queen's escape from Oxford.[1] I look back on it
now, with her son Henry II safely in the saddle,
the wild kingdom at last bridled and steadied
under his strong hand; and I can hardly believe
those evil years when it was torn in pieces between
the feeble Stephen and the dragonish Queen Matilda.
Men said then that God and his saints slept.

I served Queen Matilda for England's sake alone.
Stephen was a king too weak to rule—not the kind
to hold England together in the teeth of the
warring barons and the foreign threats. So I
followed the fierce Queen all through the war till
that long bitter winter of 1143.

That was the darkest time of all, with the tide of

[1] In the 12th century there was a long struggle for the crown
between King Stephen, grandson of William the Conqueror, and
Matilda, daughter of Henry I. It was agreed, at last that Matilda's
son, Henry, should become king after Stephen's death.

36

war against us, Stephen's troops all around Oxford, our small force hopelessly besieged, and all of us gaunt with famine. Even the river below the castle walls was frozen so a farm cart might have crossed it.

I was on sentry duty one night, pacing the wall of the castle, staring through the darkness to the winking camp fires of the enemy. My very flesh ached within the freezing metal of my armor. The frost glittered on it as I moved. There was that strange lightness that deep-fallen snow gives even on the darkest night.

Then the snow began to fall again—dizzying, soundless, a flickering curtain between me and those winking fires.

There was a movement behind me. I whirled with upraised sword.

"Quiet, man!" Sir Geoffrey's voice came low and urgent out of the darkness.

There were three of them there—two knights and

a slighter figure. It moved quite close to me, and I glimpsed the dark eyes of the Queen, huge in her starved face.

"You too," she said. "I need you with me. Another man takes your post here. The snow is our only hope."

One of the knights was already whipping one end of a long thin rope around the parapet's edge, and testing it against his weight. The other handed me a white woolen cloak. They too were all in white—

I could hardly see them between the whirling snowflakes.

"Put it on, and go first," said the Queen. "Hold the rope steady at the bottom if you can."

I stared at her through the darkness. No one loved Matilda. But when I saw her there in the freezing cold, thin and arrow straight, without a tremor at that dreadful height and the enemy lines beyond it, I knelt and kissed her hand. The next moment I had swung myself over the wall.

Those were the longest minutes of my life. The blizzard wind caught me with full force. I swung and bumped against the stone face of the castle, spinning helplessly on the twirling rope. My hands were so numb with cold that I feared every moment to lose my grip. Then, blinded and breathless, I felt the sudden thrust of the snow-covered ground

38

beneath me. It was a minute before I could stand, for all of us were weak with hunger. Then I gave a quick tug on the rope and held it steady.

It was easier for the next man, with me to hold the rope taut. Then the two of us held it, and that thin, tight slip of a woman came down it as ready and fearless as a ship's monkey. Sir Geoffrey followed and for a few minutes we crouched there in the snow, the white cloaks pulled over our heads. Even close at hand we looked no more than snowdrifts on the frozen edge of the river.

"Quick!" breathed the Queen. "Quick! This wind can't hold much longer."

It was she who led us, trusting to the blinding flurries of the snow. There came a jest and a laugh out of the darkness. We were almost on the enemy lines just at the mid point between two fires. We stopped dead, pressed down against the heaping drifts. Then came a more furious gust, and a blinding dazzle of flakes to cheat the eyes.

"Now!" whispered the Queen.

We ran. Through the lines and away behind them. Drift or snow flurry we must have seemed if anyone saw us, but no one did. Out of the bitter wind and dark, we and that fierce indomitable Queen reached safety. And now, twenty years later, her son has brought England too out of the storm.

The *Jolly Sarah*

The *Jolly Sarah* veered in a sudden gust of wind.
Clumsy as always, she swung around almost
broadside to the ridge of the oncoming wave, her
starboard deck dipping to the green swirl of the
water. Christopher held his breath. Barely her own
length separated her from the rocky point masked
with its treacherous wash of seaweed. No Port of
Spain for her, no homecoming? All her cargo of
silks and spices doomed to the salt tides?

40

But, for all her lumpishness, the *Jolly Sarah* had a kind of tough courage that many a finer ship might envy. She righted herself, shuddering as the wave struck her, seeming to pause for a long hideous moment. Then she swung again to the next gust of wind, plunged down the shining slope of water, grated lightly over the farthest edge of reef and came quietly in to the smooth harbor beyond it.

"She did it!" said Christopher. "She did it!" His face was alight with pride.

Rob nodded.

"She's wonderful. I didn't think she could. But we ought to be able to stop her swinging like that. I think she's too heavy on the starboard side."

He picked the little homemade boat out of the water and they looked at her carefully. All around them, other boys waded and chattered urging their own boats across the huge rock pool. A small wall had been built on the seaward side of it, making it a wonderful sailing pond whenever the tide left it. But Christopher and Rob, absorbed in the *Jolly Sarah*, did not notice the others.

"Do you think if we pared a bit of wood from the hull—just there . . . ?" Rob hesitated. After all, it was Christopher's boat.

"You may be right," nodded Christopher.

Heads together, they examined her closely. Christopher stroked her with a loving finger. "There *is* a bit of a bulge just there."

"Hello, Chris. Hello, Rob. What are you two up to?"

It was Christopher's father. The boy gave a little sigh. It was only when he was among others that his father took such an interest.

"We're sailing the *Jolly Sarah*," he explained. What else did his father *think* they were doing?

"It's a good pool, isn't it!" said Rob. "Some people are going to race their boats on it tomorrow."

"Oh, are they?" said Christopher's father. "That should be exciting." He took the *Jolly Sarah* from them, turning it over in his hands. "You haven't much chance of winning with this, my son."

"I'm not racing her," said Christopher. He didn't try to explain that he didn't even want to take part. Not because his boat was old and clumsy, but because she wasn't just a model like so many of the others. To him she was the ship he would sail on if she were real, the ship that went to all the places he would call at when he became a sailor himself. Cadiz, Zanzibar, Port of Spain. He knew nothing of them but their names sang inside his head. Rob understood, though he said nothing. That was why Christopher was willing to share the

42

Jolly Sarah with him. But Rob didn't know Christopher's father.

He was smiling down at them now, full of kindly enthusiasm.

"But that won't do, Chris. You must take part with the others, you know. You enter her in it."

"But I can't," said Christopher aghast. "She wouldn't have a chance. She's not in the same class as most of those. Look at them."

He gestured towards the other side of the pool, where most of the other boats clustered at that moment. Many of them were new, expensive models, with sharp clean lines and delicate balance.

"You enter your name, my boy," repeated his father firmly. "You never know your luck. I'll come down to watch."

He nodded to Rob, with what seemed oddly like a wink, and went on his way. But Christopher watched him go and made no attempt to launch the *Jolly Sarah* again.

"He will come, too," he said glumly. "You got me into it this time. And he's always disappointed if I don't win things."

For a minute he wished he had Rob's father, a casual, friendly man, who interfered very little with his son's doings. Then he thought of his own father's generosity as well as his pride in his son, and felt half ashamed. But the pleasure of the

afternoon was gone. The *Jolly Sarah* could dare no
foreign seas that day, she was just a toy boat like
the others. He wouldn't trade her for any of the
slick plastic models, but any of them would beat her
tomorrow. He parted from Rob earlier than usual.

"Lovely day for the toy boat race," was his
father's first greeting the next morning.
Christopher smiled unhappily. They went into
breakfast.

"Well," said his father with heavily simulated
surprise, "I do believe someone's left you a parcel.
Let's open it."

Christopher stared at the big oblong box beside
his plate. Any parcel is exciting, and his pulse beat
quicker. Yet he hesitated to open it.

"Go on," encouraged his father. "I want to see
what it is."

Christopher felt his eyes upon him, pleased and
hopeful, as he undid the string, opened the box,
and removed the protecting layer of cardboard
inside. He knew already what he would find.

It was a boat, even better than most of those on
the pool. It had length and elegant lines, its rigging
was beautifully made, its red plastic hull gleamed
at him with a huge self-satisfied smile. Slowly he
took it out and turned it. The name *Sunny
Christine* was clearly painted on its side.

"What about your chances in the race now, eh?" said his father, watching him.

"It's—it's beautiful, father."

"I can't let my son have anything less good than the others. You can give the old thing to Rob now, can't you?"

"No!" said Christopher sharply. He fumbled for words. "This is lovely. It was awfully kind of you to buy it for me. But the *Jolly Sarah*'s different."

"I should think she is!" said his father. "Don't be a dog in a manger, my boy. Now that you've got a fine new boat, you can surely give the other away. Let Rob have it."

He went out into the bright morning, stretching himself in the sunshine, pleased and expectant. But Christopher went back to his room, set his two boats side by side, and stared at them.

The time for the race seemed to come terribly slowly, yet all too soon. They went down to the sailing pool together in the bright windy morning. The *Jolly Sarah* was under Christopher's arm, but he carried the *Sunny Christine* carefully in both hands, trying to take the pride in her that his father expected. Rob's eyes widened when he saw her.

"What a *beauty*! Did your father give her to you? She's the best boat I've ever seen."

46

Christopher's spirits lifted suddenly. He looked at the *Sunny Christine* through Rob's eyes and saw how beautiful she was. Real pride thrilled through him.

"She *is* pretty good, isn't she? We ought to stand a chance with this."

Then Rob's eyes fell on the old wooden boat under his arm. "Are you going to sail the *Jolly Sarah* too?"

"No." Christopher remembered what his father had said. Rather slowly he held out the *Jolly Sarah*. "Perhaps you'd like to . . ." But he couldn't bring himself to say it. "Perhaps you'd like to keep an eye on her for me," he finished lamely.

"Sure." Rob took the old boat carefully and gave Christopher a quick thoughtful look. "She's a good ship too. Not as fast as some, but she's—she's solid."

Christopher nodded gratefully. Rob knew. The three of them joined the little crowd on the far side of the pool. Other boys looked with interest, and some of them with envy, at the *Sunny Christine*. For a few minutes they were all busy, testing the wind, setting the small sails, drawing lots for position. Christopher found his place was at the very end of the line. It was the side of the pool where that same jutting point of rock lurked under its patch of weed.

The starter's signal! Each little boat was pushed
forward into the wind. Christopher sent out the
Sunny Christine skillfully, on a long straight
thrust, so that the wind caught her at once. He'd
remember not to allow for the *Jolly Sarah*'s
usual swerve to starboard, and he noticed with a
sudden gleam of pleasure the long clean line that
the new boat cut in the water.

There was a tangle near the beginning. One little
ship had swerved and fouled two others. Soon
another blew to one side and grounded herself
against the rock. In a few moments there were
only two boats left in the lead—and the *Sunny
Christine* was one of them. A blue elegant little
craft drew ahead, then loitered suddenly with her

48

sail flapping. But the breeze caught the other at a slightly different angle, filling her sail and driving her forward like a gull. But just ahead was the rocky point. Without even knowing what he did, Christopher clutched at his father's arm. The *Jolly Sarah*, broad, shallow, and solid, might have done it. But could this elegant creature ever clear it with her deep narrow keel?

"Oh go *on*!" he begged her. "Go on!"

There was the slightest check and tremor, as she swept into the weed, but her own speed took her through. The next moment she was bobbing gently against the rock on the far side, and everyone was clapping.

Christopher's father was more pleased than anyone. He bought each of them a couple of ice cream cones, just to celebrate, and the *Sunny Christine* lay in full view on a corner of the table. When he left them, Christopher put the new boat down on the floor and took the *Jolly Sarah* from Rob. He knew every inch of her—the deep scratch along her paint, the little knots in the wood, that awkward bulge in the hull.

"She's an explorer's ship," said Rob, "not just a racing clipper."

Their eyes met in complete understanding. Then Christopher grinned and pushed the *Jolly Sarah* across the table.

"She's yours to keep," he said. "Come on. I'll race you back to the pool."

The flowering stone

Chisel rang upon stone with a sharp sweet sound.
White dust danced in the sunlight pouring through
the still unglazed windows of the unfinished
church. And the master mason whistled softly
between his teeth as he worked on the capital of
his pillar. It stood in strong light between two
windows, where the carving would show very clearly.
Already, roughly formed as yet, the trumpet shape
of a flower was emerging from the stone.

50

But Master John's mind was leaping ahead. His pillar would be a fine work of art. But the best of all would be the great rood screen dividing chancel from nave. He saw his own design in his mind's eye—the small foliated arches, the central cross with the two mourning figures, one on either side. He thought suddenly that his new apprentice, with his young eager face and thoughtful eyes, would make an excellent model for Saint John.

There was the sound of running feet in the aisle below. He recognized a messenger of Lord Brandon on whose orders the church was being built.

"Master John! Master John! My Lord must speak with you at once."

The mason gave one more tap with his chisel before laying it carefully down.

"Tell him I come."

He descended the ladder without haste. It was beneath the dignity of a great master mason to hurry like a servant, even at Lord Brandon's summons. He stopped, in passing, to look at the work of Stephen, the senior apprentice. Stephen's pillar was in a dim area that would be darker still when the windows were filled in. His work was sound enough if he had something to copy, but it was sometimes clumsy.

"That last leaf isn't quite right, master," said Stephen humbly. He rubbed his hand nervously down his breeches.

"It is good enough, Stephen," said Master John kindly. "You do your best, and all work is good that is done for the glory of God."

Giles, the new apprentice, was working on the capital of the next pillar. He was too absorbed to notice his master staring up in astonishment. This too was a copy. But the first leaf, already finished,

52

seemed almost alive in its delicate precision. This was no copyist, but a great artist in the making—one who could even become a rival to himself. Stephen leaned across from his own work.

"Now there's a fine piece of craft, Master John," he said admiringly. "Ay, I'll never be as good as that, I fear."

"Get back to your own work," snapped his master. He was surprised by the sudden anger that rose in him, yet unable to check it. Giles looked down at him, startled. "That stalk is too thick," he went on roughly. "Put it right before I come back."

At the door of the church he paused, still angry, yet ashamed. He heard Stephen's slow country voice.

"Eh lad, maybe he's troubled to get a message. But he'd no call to speak to thee like that. 'Tis good work."

"But he's right, Stephen. The stalk should be lighter." The boy's tone grew happier. "They say Master John's the best master craftsman in three counties. I never thought I'd have the luck to work under him."

The chisels began to ring again, busy as woodpeckers, and the mason moved away towards the manor.

The sun was already low when he returned and called his apprentices.

"I am called away from the work. My lord sends me north to the great abbey he is building there, the master mason is sick. There is no one I can put here to help you while I am gone. You must do what you can until my return. You, Stephen, will be in charge. Teach the lad to use his tools properly."

Giles flushed a little, but held his peace. He wondered what he had done to displease so much. Silently he began to put away his tools before going home.

Many weeks later, at the time of apple-ripening, Master John came back from the north. Folks greeted him as he passed through the village for he was well liked despite his pride and his fierce temper.

"You'll be going to the new church?" said one old man with a chuckle. "Ah, you'll find some surprises there, I reckon."

The mason stared at him and quickened his steps. As he approached the church he heard laughter and a young voice singing, and the familiar clink, clink of iron upon stone.

He slipped quietly, unnoticed, through the door. The apprentices were working at the far end of the church. Treading softly he went from pillar to pillar, and each time he paused the painful surge of jealousy grew stronger. Each capital had a different design of leaves and flowers, such as grew

54

in the village hedgerows. Stephen's were easily recognized, solid, workman-like, and obvious. But the others! Ivy that seemed to breathe with its own movement, honeysuckle that clung with delicate tendrils, oak leaves firm and sharply edged. And there, almost at the center of the church, in fullest light, his own pillar—the one which he had meant, next to the rood screen, to be the greatest glory of the building.

So indeed it was. The frail flowers of convolvulus, begun by his own hand, now circled the whole pillar. Trailing among their slender stalks and pointed leaves, they flowed down from the capital, casting festoons all down and around the column itself. They looked as if they might move in the first touch of wind, as if summer itself were growing inside the church.

There was a movement beside him.

"Greeting, Master John," said Stephen's voice. " 'Tis good to see thee back again."

But Giles said nothing. Wide-eyed and a little breathless—his master could still see his face as the Saint John he designed for the rood screen—he waited for a word. Master John looked from him to the pillar, the masterpiece which should have been his own, and felt the hot, blind rage rising within him. A young, untaught boy! How dared he so challenge his own skill! The jealous pain gathered to a grip on his very heart, and he snatched at the hammer that Giles held loosely in his hand. He saw the boy's eyes darken with shock and fear, felt his own muscles tensing for a blow.

Then Stephen's rumbling, quiet voice broke through the red mists that swirled inside his head.

" 'Tis a masterpiece, surely! That's what it is, a masterpiece!" His eyes on the pillar, he had not seen the other man's savage movement. " 'Tis just as you say, Master John—a work to the glory of God."

Slowly the red mists ebbed away, the hot rage cleared. Master John looked from Stephen's honest wondering gaze to Giles' pale face, and back to the splendid pillar in its shaft of light. He was a great enough artist to feel suddenly humble as he stared at its perfection.

He laid down the hammer with a rush of inward shame, and laid a quiet hand on the shoulder of each apprentice.

"*All* the work is good, and gives God glory. Men will see it here long after we are forgotten, and they will know that there were master craftsmen here in England. Tomorrow we begin work on the rood screen."

The look that he gave his young apprentice was that of one master to another. And Giles took up his tools again, whistling.

Derelict

John Fosdike lounged out, shoulders hunched, into the chilly gray afternoon. He was bored in this town where newcomers hardly seemed welcome.

At the end of the street a derelict factory building pushed black and jagged spikes up into the gathering mist. He started off in that direction, then realized too late that the gang was waiting on the next corner. His stomach pricked, and he felt his hands go clammy. Most of the boys went to the same school as he did. Some, he thought, might have been friendly. But Mike Dowd was the leader, and Mike just didn't like him.

It was too late to go back. He'd already been seen.

"Hi!" shouted Mike. "There's Johnny! Come on, Johnny. Left, right, left, right . . ."

The gang laughed. They began to sway and stamp in time to him. John hated them. He wanted to hit them, but there were too many. He could cross the road and pretend not to mind. But he did mind. And he was tired of being alone. He thrust his cold hands in his pockets and walked steadily on.

Mike swaggered out into his path, a bullying red-headed tiger of a boy.

"Hello, Johnny."

"Don't call me Johnny."

"Why not, Johnny boy. Johnny, Johnny, Johnny." The others joined in. They crowded him against the wall, chanting and laughing. "Johnny, Johnny, Johnny."

A thin-faced boy suddenly pushed one of the others aside and stood beside him.

"Leave him alone," he said. "He's new. Give him a chance." He was a boy in John's own class, and once or twice they had spoken. John liked his face.

59

Mike Doud swung around on him, glinting.

"This is *my* gang, Larry Thomas. Are you telling me what to do?"

Larry stood his ground. "Give him a chance," he repeated doggedly.

The gang was quiet, expectant. One or two boys muttered approvingly. Mike and Larry looked at each other very straight.

"All right," said Mike. "We'll give him the test. Come on, young'un."

He grabbed John's arm and pushed him forward. John struggled free, but walked with him. Larry ranged up on the other side. Around the corner they all went, some of the boys shoving and laughing. There was a sense of challenge. At the bottom of the short deserted street was a side entrance to the old factory. One gate was missing. On the other was painted in huge red letters: DANGER, KEEP OUT. The gang surged through into a weed-grown yard. Mike gave John a sudden push in the back that sent him staggering toward the crumbling wall.

The derelict building looked sinister in the cold misty half-light. Black holes of windows gaped here and there between forgotten scaffolding. A crazy fire escape swung in places right away from the wall. And in one place the wall itself had collapsed showing an inside staircase and broken floors.

"Look," said Mike. He pointed to a window three floors up. "You climb up there and come down again, and you're part of the gang. Right?"

60

John looked at him and at Larry and back at the other boys. They all stood silent, waiting. He was suddenly angry with them all, and for a moment anger overcame the coldness in his stomach. In any case, Larry was watching.

"Right," he said.

He walked to the bottom of the rusty fire escape and waited a minute, looking for the best way up. The window was twelve feet away from the nearest steps, but the scaffolding went close to it.

Suddenly Larry pushed past him and began to climb.

"I'll show you the way," he said carelessly. But he was looking at Mike.

"We both will," said Mike. "That'll make it easy for you, young Johnny."

The fire escape creaked and shivered as it took the extra weight. Mike and Larry went faster than he did. They were older, and they had climbed it before. But John kept doggedly behind them. He was level with the second floor when a rusty iron bolt snapped with the weight of the boys above him, and the crazy steps swung suddenly outwards. John was pitched off balance and clutched wildly at the steps above. Tense with fright, he looked down into the yard below. It looked terribly far away. Faces turned up to watch them were round white blurs floating in the mist.

"Look up," said Larry's voice sharply above him. "You're all right. Move to the scaffolding when you get to this bit."

John looked up. First Larry, then Mike, reached out sideways, grabbed at a cross bar of scaffolding, took a firm grip, and swung their feet over the bar below. Reaching the same place, John had a sick moment when he thought he couldn't follow. His hands seemed too cold, yet too slippery with sweat, to take tight hold. Yet somehow he did it, and a few yards traveling sideways brought him to the window on the third floor. But Mike and Larry were now above him.

"It's all right," he called. "I made it. I did it."

"All right, Johnny," called Mike. There was no sneer in his voice now, but he was looking at Larry and not at his new recruit. And he was going higher. John was close enough to see how tight his face looked, but every time Larry made a move upward, the gang leader made one too.

"Stop!" shouted John. "You're crazy. It's too high."

His own voice sounded strange to him, and the others took no notice. He felt unable to follow, unable to go back. Pressed against the wall, the black gape of the window close to his head, he watched them. Hand by hand, foot by groping foot, they went on. Each time it was Larry who made the first move.

There were calls and cheers, half-scared, from the group below. For a dizzy second he glanced down. The blurred faces huddled in groups, uncertain yet fascinated. One or two had broken away and were running back down the street, but most waited. There was no doubt now who was forcing the challenge.

62

"Stop, Larry!" he shouted again. "That's enough! Stop!"

But Larry made another step. Mike reached up, and his hand found a tread of the fire escape where it zigzagged back above them. Slowly he eased his full weight on to the new support. For seconds the rusty iron held. Then came the ugly scrape of metal against brick, a shower of dust, and the whole tread sagged and broke.

For moments that seemed like hours John clung against the wall, eyes screwed against the falling grit, hearing Mike's scream and the thud of his body as the scaffolding broke his fall. Then Larry was somehow past him leading the way back, while he followed sick and breathless. At the bottom he tried to stop, to kneel by the huddled heap on the floor, but the others grabbed and jostled him on.

"Run!" they said. "Quick! *Get out!*"

"But we've got to help him."

"I'll phone the ambulance," said Larry. "Run!"

So he ran with the others, but not toward home. In the distance he saw Larry run to a telephone booth and come out again in a minute before heading off in the other direction. In a few minutes he heard the wailing of an ambulance siren.

Half an hour later he slipped back home, washed his filthy hands and brushed his jacket before his mother came into the kitchen. Luckily she was too full of news to look at him closely.

"There's a policeman down the street at the corner house," she told him. "And an ambulance was there too. Isn't that where that red-headed boy lives? Do you know him, John? He goes to your school, I think."

"I don't *know* him," said John, almost sullenly. "I've met him."

"I wonder if we ought to ask—in case they need help?"

"We don't even know them," said John, and went up to his bedroom before she could answer.

For an hour he hung around miserably. Outside the street lamps made orange blurs, and a few black spars of the derelict factory cut across the glow reflected into the sky. There seemed to be no one around. He wondered what Larry was thinking, and whether he'd see him in school the next day. At last he could bear it no longer. He hurried down to the front door calling to his mother.

"I'm going to go ask about Mike."

"Oh, I'm glad, dear. That's kind of you. Ask if there's anything we can do."

Outside Mike's house he hesitated. A boy loitered some distance away but came no nearer. With a spurt of determination John mounted the two steps and knocked at the door. He could feel his heart beating with a heavy drag in his chest. Slow steps came down a passage. The door opened. A thin untidy woman with faded red hair looked at him almost vacantly.

"Yes?" she said.

"I came to ask," he blurted awkwardly. "My Mom said she saw an ambulance. She says can she help."

"Thanks," said the woman. "There's nothing. Nothing at all." She seemed too dazed and shocked to talk.

He wanted to go, but he persisted.

"What was it? An accident?"

"It was Mike. He fell." Her thin hand fumbled at her skirt. "They took him to the hospital."

"Is he—is he badly hurt?"

"They don't know how bad yet."

"When will they know?"

"I don't know. I don't know."

There seemed nothing more to say. He turned and went. She began to close the door behind him but called after him.

"Thank your mother. But there's nothing. Nothing."

The boy in the street was waiting. It was Larry. Sometimes John had hoped that Larry might wait for him after school. But now he looked at him and neither of them spoke. John shook his head slightly and Larry turned away. John went into his own house and shut the door.

At the end of the street the derelict stabbed its black and jagged edges into the sky.

The visitor

I can no longer keep this story to myself, so I write it down. I daren't tell it to anyone, in case I'm thought to be mad.

It all began in late April when the apple orchards were coming into bloom. Gary and I were walking through the Four Acres just to see how things looked. I must say there isn't anything much to beat our father's fruit farm in spring, when the pink-flushed grayness of the tree trunks rises smoothly into a shower of pink blossoms, and the faint honey scent of them comes on every breath of wind. The grass was still wet after rain, and a cuckoo was calling far away although it was already nearly dusk.

We were keeping our eyes open for any sign of possible trespassers. Dad doesn't mind who walks over the farm as long as they don't do damage. But there'd been several shed fires in the neighborhood recently, and some at least had been maliciously started.

It was then that I noticed a light among the trees. The Four Acres slopes down to a little stream, and there was certainly something unusual down there. I touched Gary's arm and pointed.

"That's odd," said Gary. No one's likely to get in from *that* direction."

"It's moving along the stream too," I said. "Anyway it's not a fire." We were speaking quietly in case our voices should carry.

"Perhaps it's just an evening stroller. Plenty of people like to walk here."

"But not with a flashlight, before it's dark," I said.

We began to move quietly downward toward the stream.

"I don't think it *is* a flashlight," whispered Gary. "It's too—too diffused. And sort of pale. Look, it isn't moving any more."

We were more and more puzzled. I felt increasingly that whoever it was, it was an intruder and probably up to no good. I'm the oldest and I felt responsible.

"We'll separate," I said very quietly. "I'll go straight on toward it this way, and you creep around the side and come in behind it if you can. If it's too much for us to handle by ourselves, I'll keep an eye on it while you sprint home and give the alarm. Ready?"

Gary nodded and slid away. He's a good tracker. Moving as quietly as I could and slipping behind the trees, I stalked gently down toward the stream. The light was quite steady now, and I began to realize it was very strange indeed. It glowed very faintly against the deepening dusk, but surrounding objects hardly showed in it. And it had no apparent source. I was nearly on top of it now, and there it was—just a light and nothing else.

Then I heard Gary's voice from the far side of it. He sounded a bit scared, and I didn't blame him.

70

"David, are you there? It's queer. It's just a sort of nothing."

The light gave a kind of laugh. It sounds crazy, but it really did.

"Oh yes," it said quite gently, "there's something here. Very definitely something."

I didn't *hear* the words in the ordinary way. I just knew in my mind that they were spoken. Then Gary ran to me, around the light, not through it, and caught my hand.

"What *is* it?"

I didn't know. I thought I could see movement in the thing now, hints of shape, but none of them clear enough to recognize. The unspoken voice came again and there was certainly laughter in it.

"Don't be frightened. I'm only a visitor."

"Where do you come from?" I demanded. I know I sounded angry and unfriendly, trying to hide that I was indeed frightened.

"Oh, you wouldn't know it," said the light, pleasantly. "Another star. Millions of miles from here."

I gulped. "Another star?"

"Yes, I'm really afraid you wouldn't know it. Another universe altogether, you know. Not like the moon, just on your back doorstep as it were."

Gary's hand tightened in mine. I knew he was thinking, as I was, of every space story he'd ever read or seen on TV.

"What have you come for?" His voice was a throaty squeak. "Are your people going to—to attack us?"

"Oh, my dear boy!" The unspoken voice was still amused, yet somehow terribly sad. "Will your race never grow up? Why must you always be so frightened of anything you don't understand? Of course I don't want to attack you."

I began to recover my manners with my courage.

"I'm sorry," I said awkwardly. "You see, we never really thought space people would come here. I mean, we don't even know that any of the stars *are* inhabited."

"A great many of them, my friend. Yes, indeed, a great many of them."

I stared closely at those faint hints of shape and movement, but could make nothing of them. "Please can you tell us?" I said. "Why *have* you come here?"

"Why," said the light dreamily, "because it's so beautiful, of course. As if all the starlight of the universes were clustered here like snow. Do you know how fortunate you are? I've lived a thousand years and I know nearly every galaxy within a dozen universes. But I've never been to this particular star before. And I've never, never seen anything like this!" The light trembled and glowed as if it had drawn a deep breath of delight. "Its beauty will haunt me always. I shall have to come back again. Many times. Many times."

72

"Will we see you again then?" asked Gary.

"I don't think so," said the unspoken voice. "Your people are hardly ready to make friends with us yet. They would be frightened and puzzled as you were."

"But you let *us* see you."

"I know, my dear boy, I know. But that was a mistake. I blame myself. I loitered too long, I just couldn't tear myself away. But I shall try to come back again when no one is around at all. It's better that way."

"I wish," I said impulsively, "I wish that we could really see you before you go."

The light gave a sort of quiver. There was something curving, elegant, softly beautiful, in the middle of it, then the shape was gone again.

"I'm sorry," said the voice. "It's really very difficult to see us at all in this star's atmosphere. But one day, who knows, perhaps you will come to ours—you or your sons or your sons' sons. And we will show you the beautiful things of our planet too. We will meet in peace. May it not be too long."

Suddenly it was gone. Gary and I were standing side by side in the first thin darkness of the April night. A wind stirred the apple trees, bringing down a little scented rain of pale blossoms. The first stars glimmered in the sky, and we stared at them in silence. Stars upon stars upon stars and countless more beyond the reach of sight.

Glossary

Abbey	a monastery or house ruled by an abbot
besieged	surrounded by armed forces
caldron	a huge vat made for boiling liquids
capital	the top part of a colúmn or pillar
casting	the pouring of molten metal into a mold which will shape it
chancel	the part of a church including choir and sanctuary or sacred part where the altar is
chisel	a metal tool with a cutting edge used in shaping stone or metal
convolvulus	a trailing, twining plant like the morning glory
counsel	advice
courtiers	those people who live at a royal court
derelict	falling into decay
deter	discourage or prevent; "not deterred" is to be undiscouraged or not prevented
discordant	unharmonious, not uniting because of differences
dodgem	an amusement park car ride in which the drivers can bump their cars into one another, or dodge them
doggedly	with stubborn determination

74

earthenware	pot made of clay
ebb	drain away
famine	a great shortage of food
fatal	fateful; destined to disaster
fault	weakness; imperfection; break
festoon	carved, decorative chain hanging from two points
foliated	shaped like leaves
gaunt	thin from suffering or weariness
goading	prodding to step up action
indomitable	unconquerable
late	recently
loiter	hang around, linger
lounge	to move lazily; loaf
maliciously	with intent to cause harm
manor	during the middle ages, a large area of land, governed by a lord; also the house or mansion of the lord
mason	a skilled worker who builds with stone
mist	water or moisture, almost in the form of rain, that dims or blurs; haze

molten	melted; or made liquid by heat
nave	the main part of the inside of a church
parapet	a wall made of stone on top a castle, to protect soldiers
pared	trimmed or shaved off
pillar	a post or column, usually supporting weight of a structure
precious	of great value or high price; much cherished
prostrate	stretched out flat on the floor with the face on the ground, in submission
recruit	a newcomer to a group or activity
resigned	expecting something without hope of being able to change it
rood screen	a large cross or crucifix on a screen at the entrance of the chancel of a medieval church
scaffolding	a movable platform used by workers to stand or sit on while working high off the ground
scone	a small rolled pastry cooked on a griddle
seethe	boil

sheen	brightness
sinister	bad, leading to trouble or disaster
spar	a rounded wood or metal piece used to support rigging; a mast
starboard	the right side of a ship, looking forward
swagger	a walk that shows a self-confident or boastful feeling
switchback	a track car ride at amusement parks in which the cars move up a track carried only by the speed of their downhill descent
tendril	a slender spiral coiling part of a plant, such as a vine
treacherous	unreliable; marked by hidden danger
tremor	trembling; vibration
trespasser	someone who enters someone else's property unlawfully
vast	huge
⸱eer	to change or shift direction
⸱sh	surging action of waves